THIS BOOK BELONGS TO:

_____

Sir J M Barrie

was born in Scotland in 1860.
He wrote many plays during his lifetime,
and *Peter Pan*, published in 1904,
was originally written for the stage.
He turned it into a novel,
Peter Pan and Wendy, seven years later.

Jonathan Mercer's woodcuts have been made
specially for Ladybird Classics. They are individually
hand-crafted from box-wood.

Did you know that this book is part of the J M Barrie 'Peter Pan Bequest'?
This means that J M Barrie's royalty on this book goes to help
the doctors and nurses to cure the children who are lying ill in the
Great Ormond Street Hospital in London.

Ladybird books are widely available, but in case of
difficulty may be ordered by post or telephone from:

Ladybird Books – Cash Sales Department
Littlegate Road Paignton Devon TQ3 3BE
Telephone 0803 554761

A catalogue record for this book is available
from the British Library

Published by Ladybird Books Ltd Loughborough Leicestershire UK
Ladybird Books Inc Auburn Maine 04210 USA

LADYBIRD CLASSICS

PETER PAN

by Sir J M Barrie

BARRIE'S BIRTHPLACE

Retold by Joan Collins
Illustrated by George Buchanan
Woodcuts by Jonathan Mercer

He... listened at nursery windows

THE BOY WHO
NEVER GREW UP

This is the story of Peter Pan, a boy who never grew up, but ran away to live in the Neverland when he was small. The Neverland is an island that children visit in their dreams and where anything can happen. To reach it, you have to be able to *fly*.

Peter could fly. Sometimes, when he felt lonely, he went back to the human world and listened at nursery windows to the bedtime stories mothers told their children.

Three children called Wendy, Michael and John Darling lived with their parents near Kensington Gardens. (This was one of Peter's favourite places. You can see a statue of him there.)

The children had an unusual nurse, called Nana. She was a big Newfoundland dog who slept in a kennel in the nursery. If she had been on guard the night Peter came, this story would never have happened.

Mrs Darling was a happy woman, who hugged and kissed her children often. Mr Darling was more serious. He worried a lot and did not think it was a good idea to have a dog for a nursemaid.

Mrs Darling used to tell the children bedtime stories every night. Then she tucked them in and lit their night-lights. As she tidied up the nursery, she would wonder what they were dreaming about.

If Mrs Darling could have seen into their minds, she would have seen a picture map of the island of Neverland. It had a lagoon, a pirate ship, flamingos and a coral reef. There was a forest with wild beasts, savages and fairies.

Mrs Darling was puzzled because the children talked so much about a boy called Peter Pan.

They said he 'lived with the fairies'. Mr Darling thought it must be some silly tale Nana had told them. 'It all comes from having a dog as a nurse!' he grumbled.

One day Mrs Darling found some leaves just under the nursery window. 'Peter must have dropped them,' said Wendy. 'He's so untidy!'

'But it's three floors up – how could he get here?' said Mrs Darling. 'You must have been dreaming!'

But Wendy had not been dreaming. The very next night Mrs Darling was sewing by the nursery fire and had almost fallen asleep. The window blew open, and a boy dropped in on the floor!

He was dressed all in leaves. A strange little light followed him, darting round the room like a living thing. It woke Mrs Darling, who knew at once that the boy was Peter Pan.

She cried out in alarm and Nana sprang at the boy, who leapt back through the window. Nana closed it, just catching his shadow by the feet. Nana picked up the shadow and took it to her mistress, who rolled it up and put it in a drawer.

The following Friday, Mr and Mrs Darling were invited to a party at a house a few doors away. Mr Darling was very cross with Nana, and decided she had to be chained up in the yard.

Mrs Darling was worried because Nana kept barking. 'That's not her usual bark!' she said. 'She only barks like that when there's danger!'

'Nonsense!' said Mr Darling. 'Hurry up, or we'll be late for the party!'

As the front door closed, a bright light appeared in the nursery, darting into drawers and cupboards. When the light stayed still for a moment you could see it was not a light at all, but a fairy called Tinker Bell.

The next moment Peter himself came through the window. 'Come out, Tink, wherever you are' he said, 'and show me where my shadow is!'

It was... a fairy called Tinker Bell

Tinker Bell told him it was in a drawer. She spoke in a golden tinkle, like a chime of tiny bells.

Peter pulled out his shadow and shut the drawer, forgetting that Tinker Bell was still inside. He tried to stick his shadow back on with water, then with soap, but nothing worked. He was in despair, when Wendy woke up. 'What's the matter?' she asked.

'My shadow won't stick on!' Peter complained.

'Give it to me,' said Wendy. 'I'll sew it on!'

Peter was thrilled to have his shadow back, and Wendy was so pleased that she offered him a kiss. Peter had never heard of a kiss, but he thought it must be a present so he held out his hand. Wendy gave him her thimble instead, and for ever after that, he called a kiss a 'thimble'!

In return for the thimble, Peter gave Wendy an acorn button from his coat. She put it on a chain round her neck. Later on it would save her life!

Peter told Wendy all about how he had run

away to live with the fairies in Kensington Gardens. Now he lived in the Neverland with the Lost Boys. The Lost Boys were children who had fallen out of their prams when their nurses were not looking. Nobody claimed them, so they were sent to the Neverland.

Wendy asked about the fairies.

'Once, a baby's laugh broke into a thousand pieces,' explained Peter. 'Each piece became a fairy. But now children don't believe in fairies so much. Every time a child says "I don't believe in fairies", a fairy somewhere drops down dead!'

That reminded Peter of Tinker Bell, who was still shut up in the drawer! She zoomed out in a fury, and buzzed round the room.

Wendy thought Tink was lovely, but Tinker Bell hated Wendy and was jealous of her. When Peter gave Wendy a 'thimble', Tinker Bell gave her hair a spiteful tug.

FOLLOW ME!

By now Michael and John were awake. Peter told them all about the gang of Lost Boys, of which he was the captain, and their fights with the Pirates.

'Aren't there any Lost Girls?' asked Wendy.

'No,' said Peter. 'We haven't any sisters or mothers to tell us stories and mend our clothes.'

'You poor boy!' exclaimed Wendy. 'I know lots of stories, and I could mend your clothes.'

That was just what Peter wanted – to take Wendy and her brothers back to the Neverland with him. He promised to teach them how to fly.

In the yard, Nana was barking like mad. She knew something was wrong. At last she broke her chain and galloped up to the house where the party was. She got Mr and Mrs Darling, and they all ran down the street as fast as they could.

By now Peter had blown magic dust all over the children and was showing them how to fly. 'Just wriggle your shoulders and let go!' he cried, swooping round the room. One by one, they took off from their beds and followed him.

'I flewed! I flewed!' shouted Michael.

'Look at me!' called John, bumping against the ceiling. He was wearing his Sunday top hat, and looked very funny.

'Oh, lovely!' cried Wendy, in midair.

Mr and Mrs Darling and Nana could see the nursery window lit up. Against the curtains, they saw the shadows of three little figures, circling round and round in the air. No, not three – *four*!

They rushed upstairs and burst into the room. But they were too late. Peter had said 'Follow me!' and soared out into the night with John, Michael and Wendy right behind him.

At last they saw the Neverland below

THE FLIGHT

Peter said that the way to the Neverland was easy: 'Second to the right, and straight on till morning!' But it seemed to take a very long time.

At first it was fun. The children circled round church spires and raced each other among the clouds. But as they went on, they grew tired and hungry. Peter stole food for them from the beaks of passing birds, but it was not like a proper meal.

At last they saw the Neverland below. It was just as they had imagined. They saw the lagoon, the Redskins' wigwams, and the Wild Beasts.

As they flew down through the treetops, Peter told the children about the Pirates and their dreaded leader, Captain Hook. The children had all heard of him – he was the most bloodthirsty buccaneer who had ever sailed the Spanish Main.

'I cut off his right hand!' said Peter proudly. 'Now he has an iron hook instead, and he uses it like a claw!' The children shivered.

'One thing you must promise,' Peter went on. 'If we meet Captain Hook in open fight, leave me to deal with him.' The children promised.

Just then Tinker Bell flew up, to warn them that the Pirates had loaded their big gun, Big Tom. They could tell where Peter and his friends were by Tink's light, so the children hid her in John's top hat, which Wendy carried.

Suddenly there was an enormous BANG! The gun had been fired. The blast blew them onto their backs and scattered them, and Tinker Bell and Wendy were separated from the rest.

This was Tink's great chance. She was still jealous of Wendy and wanted to get rid of her. So, with her golden tinkle, she led Wendy away in quite the wrong direction.

THE ISLAND
COMES TRUE

Now that Peter was coming back, the
Neverland came to life. The Lost Boys set out to
look for their captain, and the Pirates were
looking for the Lost Boys. The Redskins were
stalking the Pirates, and the Wild Beasts were
tracking the Redskins!

There were six Lost Boys: Tootles (the unlucky
one), Nibs (the cheerful one), Slightly (the
conceited one), Curly (was always in trouble!)
and the Twins. They crept along behind the
bushes in single file, clutching their daggers.

Then came the Pirates, with their evil looks,
some wearing gold earrings, others tattooed all
over. They had names like Cecco, Bill Jukes and

Gentleman Starkey. The worst one, because he looked so meek and mild, was Smee the Bo'sun. He had a cutlass named Jimmy Corkscrew, which he wriggled in his victims' wounds.

Their leader, Captain Jas (short for James) Hook, was the most evil rogue of all. He feared nothing except the sight of his own blood, which was an ugly colour. He treated his men like dogs and smoked two cigars at once, in a special holder.

Hook had a lean, scowling face and long black ringlets. He thought he looked like Charles II, and dressed like him. If any of his crew annoyed him, out shot his hook. There would be a tearing sound, a scream, then the body would be tossed aside. Hook was Peter Pan's greatest enemy.

On the trail of the Pirates stole the Redskins. Great Big Little Panther was their Chief, and Tiger Lily their Princess. She was a beautiful, proud maiden, as brave as any warrior.

Next came a procession of Wild Beasts;

Captain Hook was the most evil rogue of all

man-eating lions, tigers and the like, all with their tongues hanging out for food. Last of all, there came an enormous Crocodile.

The Lost Boys reached their underground home, a cave hollowed out under the roots of seven tall trees. Each trunk had a door – a hole just big enough for a boy to wriggle into. There was one door for each boy, and one for Peter Pan. So far, the Pirates had not discovered them.

Although the Pirates tried to catch Nibs as he ran away, Hook held them back. 'One is no good!' he said. 'I want all of them!' And he sat down to wait while the Pirates searched the wood.

As he sat, Hook told Smee how Peter Pan had cut off his hand. 'He threw it to a passing crocodile,' Hook snarled. 'It liked the taste so much that it has followed me ever since, licking its lips for the rest of me! Luckily it also swallowed a clock. It goes *tick, tick, tick,* so I can hear it coming and escape!'

'One day,' said Smee, 'the clock will run down!'

'That's what I'm afraid of,' said Hook.

Just then, a familiar sound reached Hook's ears.

Tick, tick, tick, tick – it was the Crocodile!

Hook and Smee dashed away, and the boys came out of hiding. Nibs rushed back, pointing up at the sky. Something like a great white bird was floating their way. They didn't know that it was actually Wendy in her nightie.

Tinker Bell was flying all around her, pinching her. Wendy was moaning 'Poor Wendy!' to herself.

'Peter wants you to shoot the Wendy bird!' Tink called to the boys.

The boys always did what Peter wanted, so they hurried away for their bows and arrows. Tootles was the first back. 'Quick, Tootles, quick!' Tink screamed. 'Peter will be so pleased!'

Tootles fitted an arrow to his bow and fired. Wendy fluttered to the ground, the arrow in her heart.

21

'She is dead,' said Peter

THE LITTLE HOUSE
AND THE
HOME UNDERGROUND

When the boys crowded round to see the Wendy bird, they discovered to their horror that it was a lady.

'A mother to take care of us,' said the Twins, 'and Tootles has shot her.'

It was all part of Tootles' bad luck. He would have run away if Peter hadn't arrived.

'I've brought you all a mother,' he said joyfully. 'Haven't you seen her? She flew this way.'

The Lost Boys stood aside and showed him Wendy.

'She is dead,' said Peter. 'Who shot her?'

'I did,' Tootles confessed. 'Now kill me.'

Peter was raising the arrow to strike, when Nibs shouted, 'The Wendy lady moved her arm!'

'Poor Tootles!' Wendy moaned.

'She's alive!' Peter cried. He knelt down and saw that the acorn button he gave her had stopped the arrow and saved her life.

'Listen to Tink!' said Curly. 'She's crying because Wendy's not dead.'

When the boys told Peter what Tinker Bell had done, Peter was furious. 'I am no longer your friend, Tinker Bell,' he said. 'Go away for ever!'

Wendy moved her arm again.

'Well,' said Peter, 'go away for a week, then.'

Tinker Bell wasn't the least bit grateful to Wendy. She just flew away, as cross as two sticks.

The Lost Boys didn't know what they should do for Wendy. They couldn't carry her down into the cave.

'I know!' said Peter. 'We'll build a little house all round her!'

The boys rushed off to fetch branches, bedding and firewood, and Michael and John helped.

Bit by bit the house was built, with a green moss carpet, red walls, and a door and windows. At last all it needed was a chimney. Peter knocked the top out of John's Sunday hat and fitted it on the roof. It began to smoke at once!

'This is your own little house!' said Peter.

'And we are your children!' said the Lost Boys.

The cave where Peter and the boys lived was one enormous room. There was a huge bed slung against the wall, which was let down at night. The Lost Boys slept in it like sardines in a tin.

Tinker Bell had her own tiny room, elegantly furnished with a couch, a dressing-table and a mirror. There was even a crystal chandelier.

Wendy did all the cooking for the boys. They ate island food – roast pig, breadfruit and bananas. Wendy liked to sit by the fire at night, when the boys were asleep, darning their socks.

The mermaids lazed on the rocks

THE MERMAIDS'
LAGOON

At the edge of the island there was a vivid
blue lagoon where mermaids swam. The
mermaids lazed on the rocks, combing their long
hair and splashing the children with their tails if
they came too near. On moonlit nights they sang
strange wailing songs, and on those nights it was
dangerous to go near the lagoon.

A Never-bird had built her nest in one of the
trees by the shore and laid six eggs in it. One day
the nest fell and floated out on the lagoon. The
mother bird still sat there, drifting about in her
nest like a little boat. Peter warned the boys to
be careful not to disturb her.

There was a huge black rock out at sea, which

was covered with water at high tide. Pirates used to tie up their captives and leave them there to drown, so it was called Marooners' Rock.

One afternoon, when Wendy and the boys were having a nap on the Rock, the sun went in, and the lagoon became cold and unfriendly. Wendy tried not to be afraid, even when she heard the sound of a boat approaching.

Peter, always on the alert, smelled danger. 'Pirates!' he cried. 'Everybody dive!'

The next moment, the Rock was empty.

The pirate dinghy, rowed by Smee and Starkey, drew near. They had captured Tiger Lily just as she was boarding the pirate ship with a knife between her teeth. They had tied her hands and feet and were going to leave her on the Rock to drown. She showed no fear, for she was a chief's daughter.

Peter wanted to save Tiger Lily and have some fun as well. 'Ahoy, you lubbers!' he called, imitating Hook's voice. 'Set the Redskin free!'

'But Captain,' said Smee, 'you told us…'

'At once, d'you hear,' cried Peter, 'or I'll plunge my hook in you!'

'Better do what the Captain orders,' muttered Starkey nervously. So they cut Tiger Lily's ropes and she slipped like an eel into the sea.

Suddenly a cry came across the water. 'Boat ahoy!' It was the real Captain Hook, swimming out to join his men. He had come to talk about a plan to capture Peter and his gang.

'We may never get the better of those boys now they have a mother to care for them!' he said.

'I know,' said Smee. 'But if we capture her, she can be *our* mother!'

'A capital idea!' cried Hook. 'But first we must catch the boys and make them walk the plank!'

Hook was furious to find that his men had let Tiger Lily go. 'I gave no such orders!' he said.

When they told him about the mysterious

voice, Hook was frightened. 'Spirit that haunts this dark lagoon,' he called, 'dost hear me?'

Peter could not keep quiet. 'Odds, bobs, hammer and tongs, I hear you!' he called.

'Who are you, stranger?' asked Hook hoarsely.

'I am James Hook, Captain of the *Jolly Roger*!'

'If you are Hook, then who am I?'

'You're a codfish!'

Hook went pale at this insult. He knew now who was playing this trick on him. 'Are you a boy?' he called. 'Are you a *wonderful* boy?'

'Yes, yes!' boasted Peter. 'I am! I'm Peter Pan!'

At once Hook ordered his men to attack. 'Take him, dead or alive!' he cried.

Peter whistled up the boys, and they all came to his aid, armed with daggers. They put up a good fight. Before long, Smee and Starkey were swimming for their lives towards the pirate ship.

Peter had ordered the boys to leave Hook to him, so they rowed for shore in the pirate dinghy.

They put up a good fight

Peter and Hook came out of the water at the same moment. They stared grimly at one another as they climbed onto the Rock, and Peter snatched a knife from Hook's belt. Then, seeing that Hook was lower down than he was, Peter gave him a hand up, so they could fight fairly. But the treacherous Hook bit Peter's hand. Peter was so shocked that he dropped his guard, and Hook was able to claw him twice.

The tide was rising rapidly, so Hook struck out for his ship, leaving Peter wounded. As the tide rose, Peter's heart beat like a drum. A strange smile came over his face, and he thought, 'To die will be an awfully big adventure!'

But Peter did not die. The Never-bird came by in her nest and rescued him. When he returned to the cave, he saw campfires. The Redskins had come to protect the boys from Pirate attack. Peter had saved Tiger Lily, and there was nothing they would not do for him and his friends.

WENDY'S STORY

Safe inside their cave, the children sat round for a make-believe tea. They were so excited that Wendy decided to settle them down with a story.

She began to tell a story that Peter hated. It was about three children who had a nurse called Nana, and how they flew away one night, and how their father and mother missed them. 'Think how sad they were when they saw the empty beds!' she said.

Then she came to the part that Peter hated most. She told them how much mothers love their children. 'The mother always left the window open for the children to fly back in. So they stayed away for years and had a lovely time.'

Peter was very upset. 'Wendy, you're wrong

about mothers!' he said. Then he told them what had happened when *he* went back home. 'I thought, like you, that my mother would always keep the window open for me. So I stayed away a long time. But when I flew back, my mother had forgotten me. The window was shut, and there was another little boy in my bed!'

Michael and John began to cry, afraid that their mother might forget them too. They begged Wendy to take them home. The Lost Boys said they wanted to come too, and Wendy promised she would ask Mr and Mrs Darling to adopt them.

Peter was very hurt, but he was too proud to show it. And he would not make Wendy stay against her will. 'I will ask the Redskins to show you the way through the wood, and Tinker Bell can guide you when you fly over the sea,' he said, stoutly.

'But aren't you coming too?' asked Wendy.

They begged Wendy to take them home

'Oh, no!' exclaimed Peter. 'They would make me grow up! I want to stay a little boy always, and have fun!'

Then Peter and Wendy shook hands – Peter did not even give Wendy a 'thimble'. Wendy measured out a dose of his medicine (it was only water), and put the glass next to his bed. 'Promise me you'll take it,' she said in a motherly way.

'I promise. Now lead the way, Tinker Bell!' he ordered.

Tink darted up the nearest tree, but nobody followed her. For it was at that moment that the Pirates made their dreadful attack on the Redskins. The air was full of shrieks and howls and the clash of steel!

Below, there was dead silence. Wendy fell to her knees, and the boys turned to Peter, holding out their arms and begging him not to desert them.

Peter seized his trusty sword, ready to do battle.

THE CHILDREN ARE
CARRIED OFF

Hook and his fiendish crew had taken the
Redskins by surprise, so the Pirates had a mean
advantage. Almost the whole Redskin tribe
perished. Only the Chief, Tiger Lily and a few
warriors managed to fight their way out.

But Hook's work was not yet over. There was
hatred in his wicked heart for Peter Pan.

Hook knew that if the boys heard the
Redskins' tom-tom, they would come out of
hiding, thinking the Redskins had won. So he
signalled to Smee, who beat the tom-tom twice.

'It's a Redskin victory!' cried Peter.

The boys cheered and got ready to leave the
cave, saying a last goodbye to Peter.

As they came up, one by one, each was caught by a Pirate and trussed up like a chicken.

Then the Pirates bundled the children into the little Wendy House and carried it on their shoulders to the *Jolly Roger*.

Hook was left behind. He looked carefully at the trees and discovered that one of them was more hollow than the others. He could just squeeze in. He could not open the door, but he peered through a chink and saw Peter lying peacefully asleep on the great bed. For a moment his cold heart was touched. Then he spied Peter's medicine, which he could just reach.

Hook always carried a deadly poison on him. Reaching through the chink, he poured five drops into Peter's medicine.

Then he climbed out of the tree like some evil spirit. Pulling his hat over his eyes, he wrapped his black cloak around him and stole away through the wood.

Each was caught by a pirate

DO YOU BELIEVE
IN FAIRIES?

At ten o'clock that night, Peter was awakened
by a tiny knock on the door. It was Tinker Bell,
who told him that Wendy and the boys had been
captured and taken to the Pirate ship.

'I'll rescue them!' cried Peter, grabbing his
sword. 'But first I must take my medicine!'

'No! No!' cried Tinker Bell. 'It's poisoned!'

'How could it be?' said Peter. 'Nobody has
been down here.' He put the glass to his lips. But
brave Tinker Bell had heard Hook talking to
himself in the wood, and flew between Peter's
mouth and the glass. She drank the poison herself,
in one gulp.

'It *was* poisoned!' she cried. 'I shall die!'

She fluttered feebly to her tiny couch and lay there gasping. Her light was getting weaker every moment. Soon it would go out.

Tink was whispering something. Peter bent down to listen. 'If enough children believe in fairies,' she gasped, 'I might get better again!'

What could Peter do? Children everywhere were asleep. Then he thought of those who were dreaming of Neverland. He called, 'If you believe in fairies, *clap your hands*! Don't let Tink die!'

There was silence. Then there was a faint sound of clapping. It grew and grew until it filled the cave. Tink was saved! Her voice grew strong and she flashed round the room, as merry as ever.

'And now to rescue Wendy!' cried Peter.

He came up through the tree into the moonlit wood. No one was about, except for the Crocodile, which never slept, passing down below.

Peter swore a terrible oath: 'It's Hook or me this time!'

'Have you any last messages for your children?'

THE FIGHT ON THE PIRATE SHIP

Aboard the *Jolly Roger*, Hook had the boys dragged up from the hold. He promised to spare two of them if they would join the crew.

'Would we be free subjects of the King?' asked John, bravely.

'You would have to swear "Down with the King!" ' growled Hook.

'Then we say *No*!' was the answer.

'Bring out the plank!' roared Hook. 'And fetch their mother!'

Wendy was brought up to see her boys walk to their death in the briny ocean.

'Have you any last message for your children?' sneered Hook.

Wendy spoke out firmly: 'All your mothers hope you will die bravely like true Englishmen!'

'Tie her to the mast!' Hook screamed.

The boys' eyes were on the plank. It was the last walk they would ever take. There was a grim silence – but it was broken by a strange sound: the *tick, tick, tick* of the Crocodile!

Hook collapsed with fear. He crawled along the deck, crying to his men, 'Hide me! Hide me!'

As the crew gathered round Hook, the boys looked over the side and saw – not the Crocodile, but Peter Pan! *He* was ticking! Signalling to the boys not to give him away, he slipped aboard and ran to hide in the Captain's cabin.

When the ticking stopped, Hook grew brave again. He lined up the boys for a flogging and sent Jukes to his cabin for the cat-o'-nine-tails.

Jukes entered the dark room. Suddenly there was a terrible scream; a blood-chilling crow followed. Jukes had been killed by Peter!

Two more Pirates suffered the same fate.

After this the crew lost their nerve, and no one else would venture forth. So Hook sent in the eight boys. 'Let them kill each other!' he snarled.

This was just what Peter wanted. He unlocked the boys' chains with a key he had found, and armed them with Hook's weapons. Then, while the Pirates' backs were turned, they all crept out on deck. Peter freed Wendy and, wrapping himself in her cloak, took her place at the mast. Then he let out a terrific '*Cockadoodle-doo!*'

The Pirates, frightened out of their wits, spun round. ''Tis an unlucky ship,' they cried, 'that has a captain with a hook!'

''Tis because we have a woman on board,' said Hook quickly. 'Fling her over the side!'

'No one can save you now, missy!' said one of the kinder Pirates sadly.

'Here's one who can!' cried Peter, throwing aside the cloak. 'Peter Pan!'

A great fight began. Swords and cutlasses clashed, and bodies tumbled into the water. Soon only Hook was left. His sword flashed like a circle of fire.

'Leave him to me, boys!' cried Peter.

Although he was smaller, Peter was nimbler and soon wounded Hook. At the sight of his own blood, Hook turned pale and dropped his sword. He rushed to set fire to the powder magazine and blow the ship up. But Peter bravely snatched the torch from his hand and threw it into the sea.

Hook backed away from the menacing Peter and climbed on the bulwark. Peter aimed a kick at him, and Hook lost his balance, slithering straight down into the sea.

The Crocodile, whose clock had run down at last, had silently followed Peter and was waiting patiently below. As Hook reached the water, the Crocodile opened his jaws – and finally had the rest of Hook for his supper.

'Leave him to me, boys!'

THE RETURN HOME

That night the boys slept in the Pirates' bunks, and next morning they set off for home, with Peter as captain.

Meanwhile, Mr and Mrs Darling were still grieving over their lost children. Mr Darling was sure it was all his fault for chaining up Nana, and, to punish himself, he slept in her kennel.

One night he was feeling especially miserable, so he asked Mrs Darling to play the piano in the room next door to cheer him up. 'And please shut the window,' he said. 'It's draughty in the kennel.'

'You know I can't do that, dear!' said Mrs Darling. 'The children might come home!'

But the children were already on their way!

They had crossed the sea now and were flying the last bit of the way. Peter and Tinker Bell were ahead of the others, as Peter had a plan. When they found the open window and flew in, Peter was going to shut the window, so that Wendy would think her mother had forgotten her, and go back with him to the Neverland.

But Mrs Darling was sitting sadly at the piano, with tears trickling down her face.

'She is fond of Wendy too!' thought Peter miserably. 'We can't *both* have her. What had I better do?' Then he gave in and said, 'Oh, come on, Tink. We'll let them in.'

So Wendy and Michael and John slipped into the nursery. They decided to get into bed and pretend they had never been away.

When Mrs Darling came in and saw that the beds were full, she thought it was a dream! Then the children spoke to her. She put her arms round them, woke her husband and called Nana.

He was looking... at the one joy he could never share

Peter Pan had had many strange experiences that other children could never know, but now he was looking through the window at the one joy he could never share.

The Darlings adopted the Lost Boys, and Mrs Darling let Wendy go back to the Neverland once a year to help Peter with the spring-cleaning.

Peter came back to visit Wendy too. He had not much idea of time, so he did not come every year. Once he left it so long that when he next came, Wendy was grown up and had a little girl of her own, called Jane.

You can guess what happened. Jane wanted to go back with him, and Wendy let her.

As Peter never grew up, one year Jane's *daughter* was the one who went. And so it will go on, as long as there are children, and the Neverland, and Peter Pan!

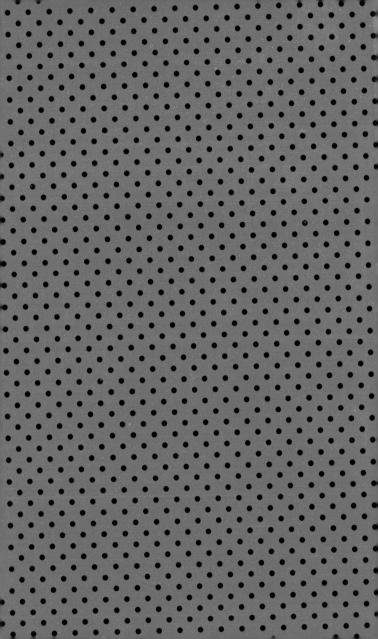